P9-BHW-123

Houghton Mifflin Company  Boston  1979

JP
M

Library of Congress Cataloging in Publication Data

Marshall, James, 1942-
  Portly McSwine.

  SUMMARY: Despite all attempts to reassure him,
Portly McSwine frets about the National Snout Day
celebration he has planned.
  [1.  Pigs—Fiction.  2.  Parties—Fiction]
I.  Title.
PZ7.M35672Po     [E]     78-24814
ISBN 0-395-28003-6

For Adolph Garza
and
Modesto Torre

Portly McSwine gazed out the window.
National Snout Day was only a day away,
and Portly was planning a huge party.
"Oh dear," he said. "I've
never given a party before."

At his office McSwine couldn't concentrate on his work.
"Stop worrying," said Esther his secretary. "You'll make yourself sick."

After work Portly had
a troubling thought.
"Oh my," he said. "What
if I should get sick?"
He imagined how disappointed
his party guests would be.

Portly decided to stop at the
doctor's for a flu shot.
"Quit fretting," said the doctor.
"I'm sure your party will
be very amusing."

Outside the doctor's Portly
stopped short.
"Oh golly," he said. "What
if my party isn't amusing
enough?"
He imagined his guests
groaning with boredom.

People on the street couldn't
help noticing that
Portly was talking to himself.
He was rehearsing his most
amusing stories to tell at the party.

In front of the fudge shop
Portly ran into his old friend
Emily Pig.
"Will there be refreshments
at the party?" asked Emily.
"But of course," said Portly.

Stopping for a rest, Portly
had a disturbing idea.
"Oh gracious," he said. "What
if my refreshments aren't
tasty enough?"
He imagined his guests all
hopping mad and complaining.

Portly decided to stop at the baker's.
"I want to make sure my refreshments
are the tastiest in town," he said.
"Quit fussing," said the lady behind
the counter.

A block from home
Portly ran into Emily again.
"Will there be dancing at
the party?" asked Emily.
"Certainly," replied Portly.

That night Portly had
difficulty sleeping.
"Oh, Oh," he said. "What if my
dancing isn't up to snuff?"
He could imagine his guests all
*screaming* with laughter.

Portly jumped out of bed and
turned on his gramophone.
He practiced waltzing
around the living room
until he was sure his
dancing was perfectly fine.

The next day Portly's palms
began to sweat.
"My party is *tonight*!" he gasped.
"Stop upsetting yourself," said
Esther his secretary. "I'm
sure *Everyone* will have a
wonderful time."

Portly went home, put up
the party decorations, put on
his fancy party clothes, and
sat down to wait.
"What if *no* one comes?" he said.
Just then the doorbell rang.

All the guests arrived at once.
"Party time!" they shouted.
And they headed for the refreshment
table.

"The French pastry is
delicious!" squealed Emily.
"This is the best National
Snout Day party *Ever*!"
cried another guest.
Everyone seemed to be
having a wonderful time.

Portly danced with Esther.
"You see," said Esther, "there
was nothing to worry about.
I can hardly wait until next
year's party."

The following day Portly McSwine
gazed out the window.
National Snout Day was only
three hundred and sixty-four
days away, and Portly
was planning a huge party.
"Oh dear," he said. "What if
next year's party isn't so good
as this year's? Oh dear, Oh dear."